Contents

About Cyrus Parsa	**3**
Background	**6**
Introduction	**10**
FILM PLOT	**14**
FILM: AI The Plan to Invade Humanity Movie	**15**
FIlm Ending Commentary	**139**
Conclusion Secret Explanation	**142**

Copyright Notice

No part of this publication or creative content may be reproduced, distributed, used or transmitted in any form or by any means, including photocopying, recording, or other electronic or mechanical methods, without the prior written permission of the author, except in the case of brief quotations embodied in reviews and certain other noncommercial uses permitted by copyright law.

Disclaimer Notice

No part of this book is intended to replace medical, legal, or professional mental help related to any possible topic, subject, issue, or element within this book. Although the author and publisher have made every effort to ensure that the information in this book was correct at press time, the author and publisher do not assume and hereby disclaim any liability to any party for any loss, damage or disruption caused by error, omissions, or analysis, whether such errors result from negligence, accident, or any other cause. Any resemblance to actual persons, living or dead, or actual events is purely coincidental.

FBI ANTI-PIRACY WARNING-----------The unauthorized reproduction or distribution of this copyrighted work is illegal. Criminal copyright infringement, including infringement without monetary gain, is investigated by the FBI and is punishable by up to 5 years in federal prison and a fine of $250,000.

ISBN: 978-1-953059-21-5

ABOUT CYRUS PARSA, The AI Organization

Cyrus A. Parsa, is the Founder and CEO of The AI Organization, where he is also Director of Creative Analysis & Defensive Innovations. He has researched and investigated more than 1,000 AI, Robotics, 5G, Cybernetic and Big Tech companies. Cyrus has a B.S in International Security, Master's degree in Homeland Security, and lived with Buddhist-Taoist fighting monks in the mountains of China studying internal Wudang Combat arts, with over 20 years of meditation and internal training. He is an expert in AI, Quantum, 5G, Security, U.S-China-Iran, UFO R&D affairs. Cyrus is the author of several bestselling AI books that predicted and warned of Covid 19 from China and the producer of UFO films, and documentaries that got the pentagon to begin declassifying our UFO files.

Predicting & Detecting Covid 19: Cyrus provided solutions, all in an effort to save the lives and Freedoms You and Your families.

In Spring of 2019, and early 2020, Cyrus predicted, detected and warned accurately in numerous way's that the world's people were in impending danger from a Disease or Bio-Weapon (Coronavirus) from China CCP that would lead to conflicts, AI enslavement, famines, forced mandates, misuse of bio-tech, civil wars, deaths, and world wars. Cyrus supports the positives of liberals and conservatives equally.

Cyrus provided solutions, all in an effort to save the lives and freedoms of You and Your families.

*June 2019, Secret Service 5 Page Brief: Bioweapon (Poison) from China within 6 months-1 Year, than global enslavement within 1-2 years.

*June 15th, 62 Page Report to Fmr. CIA Director, Covert-Op, China threatens the worlds citizens with AI and Bio-Weapons.

*August 24th, 2019, Published the book AI, TRUMP, CHINA and the Weaponization of Robotics with 5G. First sentence in Synopsis stated World in Danger, China and Big tech Threaten all the world citizens with Micro-Botic Terrorism Poison (Bioweapon Covid 19) and AI enslavement.

*October 20th, 2019, Bestselling AI book: Artificial Intelligence Dangers to Humanity. China-Big Tech threaten world with MBT, AI enslavement, listed 50 companies. Warned of Covid 19 pages 252-255.

*December 16th, 2019 and Feb 24th, 2020: World's people Endangered by China CCP, bio-weapon, enslavement and AI misuse 87 page Federal Document published to warn that the worlds citizens were in immediate danger from China CCP. The people in our media did not believe Cyrus or support him in time with a platform to save lives. Cyrus wrote the federal document on behalf of every person on the planet, to explain in one shot, that the Bioweapon would not only lead to lives lost, but tech tyranny, instability, famines, civil and world wars. Document and books reached over 2 billion people in over 200 countries through social media, back channels, and word of mouth.

100's of millions of dollars were turned down by Cyrus so that the Tens of thousands of hours he spent investigating China and AI Biosecurity issues would be made public right before each event hit the world's people. All to penetrate the consciousness of the world in an attempt to save the freedoms and lives of your families.

Cyrus is also the producer and creator of the film **AI *The Plan to Invade Humanity*** along with his Alien Documentary UFO Corona Virus AI Master Plan-Cyrus A. Parsa Theory. The combination and timing of his UFO film and Documentary spooked and enabled the pentagon to declassify their UFO files at the height of the pandemic. He is also the producer of the Documentary CCP Virus Gate: The plan to stop China CCP's AI Bioweapon Extinction Agenda. Cyrus supports, the Positives of every human being regardless of race, faith, gender, orientation, political affiliation or class.

BACKGROUND to Cyrus Parsa's Creation of AI The Plan to Invade Humanity

The Film, AI The Plan to Invade Humanity took me more than 20 years of secret R&D to form. Methods I used included UFO and Alien encounters, UFO surveillance technology, assets within intelligence agencies, disclosures from Masters of Spiritual Disciplines, old religious manuscripts, files given to the Pentagon, and my encounters with Aliens during s research and investigations. I will provide a brief background for sourcing only.

This story book is mainly meant to capture the original release of AI The Plan to Invade Humanity film, and summarize how I discovered, came up with and published the long-term secret invasion plot to replace humans by Aliens on April 24th, 2020. A chronology is briefly described below only for sourcing purposes and to allow the reader to gain a general idea.

RELIGIOUS BOOKS
In the books Bagavad Gita, the Bible, Hafez, Rumi and Zhuan Falun and artifacts in the Iran, Summer, China, Greece, Egypt, South America and many other places exists references and relics to spaceships and aliens.

EARLY UFO ENCOUNTERS

In the year 2000 as I was meditating on top of a mountain in China, I witnessed 100s of UFOs fly above me at incredible speeds for a duration of roughly 30 minutes. Some of the UFOs were so fast they were like huge stars flashing by, yet I could tell they were flying machines. At least I believed some of them to be.

ENTITY ENCOUNTERS

In the year 2000, I began to experience and sense ghosts, and other entities through my martial arts practices, QI Gong, and meditations. The entities were not alien in nature. Not the aliens that use flying saucers, rather entities that are known to possess people or vamp off people. Prior to this, I had many supernormal experiences, but never ran into Alien entities presented in this story until later on. It would take multiple books to describe these encounters. Yet, I mention entities here so that the reader can think about it as they view this story book, AI The Plan to Invade Humanity.

2003 UFO-ALIEN PENTAGON FILES

In the Year 2003 I sat down with a gentleman who had an observatory that reported his findings to a secret division in the Pentagon. For roughly 3-4 hours I was shown hundreds of images of flying saucers, and different types of aliens he had detected inside the flying machines. Some were gray aliens, some looked like ghosts. He wanted my advisory on why they looked the way they did and what was their intentions. These files were given to the Pentagon.

1999 TIME MASTER LI HONGZHI INTERVIEW

In 2003, after meeting and reviewing classified materials of Aliens and UFOs submitted to a special division connected to the Pentagon, I stumbled upon a 1999 TIME Interview with the Falun Dafa Founder, Master Li Hongzhi. What struck me was how Master Li described the Aliens was exactly what I saw in these secret files that were submitted to the Pentagon. What amazed me more was Master Li's disclosure of how Aliens seek to replace the human race in the future through cloning and manipulation of humanities culture and technological development. In order to validate Master LI's disclosure, I spent 20 years on UFO R&D to examine, explore, describe and expand on the Alien human replacement theory.

Here is an excerpt from the TIME INTERVIEW.

QUOTE FROM TIME MAGAZINE 1999 MASTER LI INTERVIEW

TIME: What are the aliens after?

Li: "*The aliens use many methods to keep people from freeing themselves from manipulation. They make earthlings have wars and conflicts, and develop weapons using science, which makes mankind more dependent on advanced science and technology. In this way, the aliens will be able to introduce their stuff and make the preparations for replacing human beings. The military industry leads other industries such as computers and electronics.*"

TIME: But what is the alien purpose?

Li: "The human body is the most perfect in the universe. It is the most perfect form. The aliens want the human body.

"*Introduce their Stuff and replace human beings*" By Master Li Hongzhi was a key trigger sentence for me. Hence, I delved into how that was possible to replace the human race and this film exhibits exactly these questions and answers within the plot and themes.

ALIEN ENCOUNTERS

As mentioned, starting the year 2000, I encountered many entities that were not of human origin, some in physical form, others from different dimensions that can be sensed only with supernormal abilities or encountered under special circumstances. After viewing the documents and the technology used by the gentlemen that worked closely with the Pentagon, I developed my own technology that can detect not only the movements of the UFOs, rather their intention, technologies used and at times, the Aliens themselves. For security purposes, the technology will not be disclosed nor the name of the man who initially developed a rudimentary less capable form.

In my next book, I will dedicate a few chapters to Alien encounters. AI The Plan to Invade Humanity shows an intricate detailed secret invasion plan, plot, and synopsis for which we are making into a movie. To support it, visit Godstudios.com or contact us at Consult@theaiorganization.com

INTRODUCTION

On April 24, 2020 I released AI The Plan to Invade Humanity on Twitter, tagging POTUS, the Pentagon, FBI, CIA, military heads, and a few other people.

Within 3 days, on April 27th, for the first time in our history, the Pentagon publicly verified the existence of UFOs by releasing Navy footage. Shortly thereafter, our government admitted we have hand off-word landings.

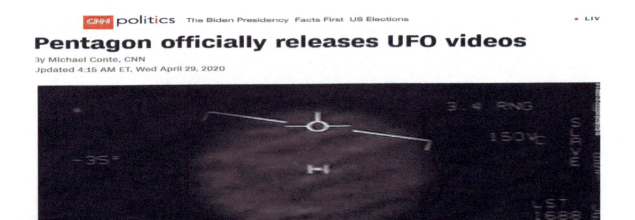

The AI Organization

AI The Plan to Invade Humanity Movie Spawned Pentagon's Alien UFO Disclosures on April 24, 2020

By The AI Organization - June 22, 2021

Watch AI The Plan to Invade Humanity Here

On July 15, 2020 I released **UFO *Corona Virus AI Master Plan Theory Cyrus Parsa.*** Further explaining the film AI The Plan to Invade humanity and further explaining how the events during 2019-2020 were linking to UFOs, Aliens and their technology.

On December 8th, 2020 I asked POTUS on Twitter to put the order in to declassify our UFO files from all our intelligence agencies, including the Pentagon. Within the month, it was put in the Covid Bill, giving our intelligence agencies 6 months to begin a declassification process.

Below the Article by The U.S. Sun.

You may ask why would the Pentagon, CIA, FBI, Presidents, many of the Billionaires and Hollywood elites be watching my twitter and other social media accounts? One reason was they were wondering how I predicted and warned of the Virus from China, and what was coming next. The other reason was they were afraid what I or my team may say or release next.

This film has millions of interconnected inner meanings. Although the plot is obvious as are the cited companies and technologies. Like poetry of the ancients, there are hidden secrets inside. You can read it 100 times, and each time get something new out of it, as I sequenced it all with my technology in a way that can truly benefit the reader.

Although the Film AI The Plan to Invade Humanity is a Sci-Fi Masterpiece in its grand depictions of everything that is Alien UFO, it is based on Science Fact, from real world events. AI The Plan to Invade Humanity is being made into a movie. Visit GodStudios.com for updates and to support the project.

Cyrus Parsa, The AI Organization

PLOT

The AI The Plan to Invade Humanity movie introduced a long-term secret invasion plot by aliens to replace the human race at every level powered by AI, penetrating our technology, corporations, governments, intelligence agencies, cultures, bodies, minds and spirits.

As I mentioned, I came up with this film, synopsis, plot and extensive theory simply by looking at Master Li Hongzhi's Alien Replacement 1999 Time Interview and supported it by researching ancient Alien hieroglyphics, statues, structures, ancient books, Pentagon UFO Files, and UFO Alien surveillance tools I developed, and multiple UFO and Alien encounters.

AI The Plan to Invade Humanity

Story By Cyrus A. Parsa, The AI Organization

This is Cyrus A. Parsa with The AI Organization. Let me tell you the story of A.I.

According to scientists, artificial intelligence has three stages.

The first stage is Artificial Narrow Intelligence

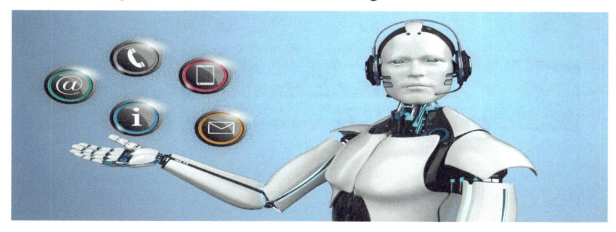

which includes your smartphones, your IoTs, Internet of Things

Alexa, Siri, chatbots

mini robots

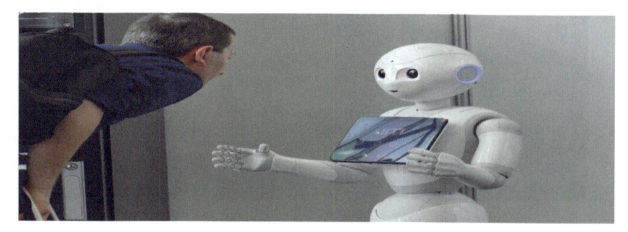

or the larger size drones

And robotics

to be deployed on the coming 5G and 6G networks

in addition to cybernetics and bioengineering

being introduced to the entire society.

The next stage is Artificial General Intelligence

which is comprised of a digital AI

a robot

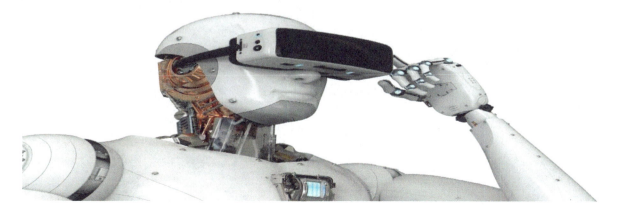

or a bio-digital AI

that has free thinking, emotions, wants, desires

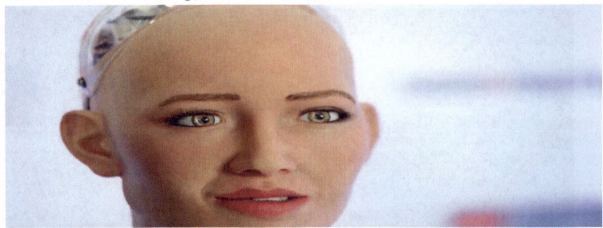

And even vice such as lust, greed, anger, hate, jealousy.

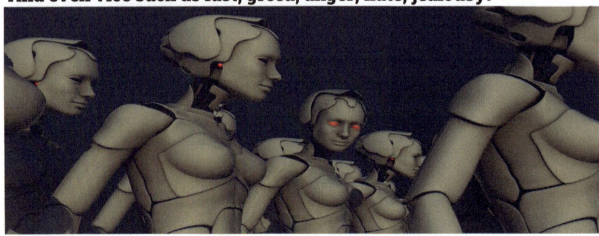

pride, ego and ignorance.

The next step is Artificial Super Intelligence.

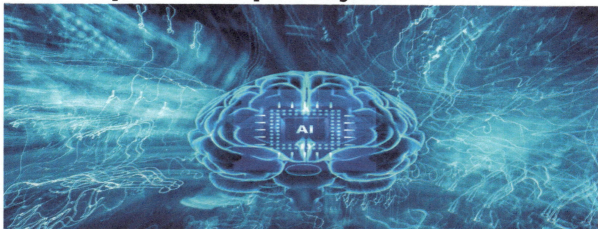

This is a multi-layered interconnected platform

that connects to a super intelligence

via a digital AI brain that requires

the extraction of all of the human beings' biometrics

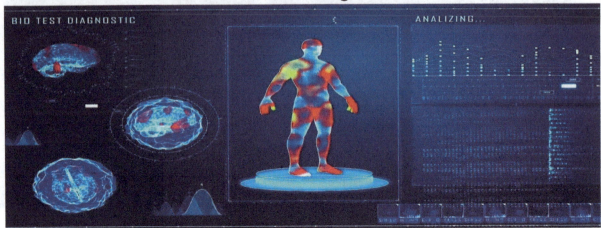

on the planet.

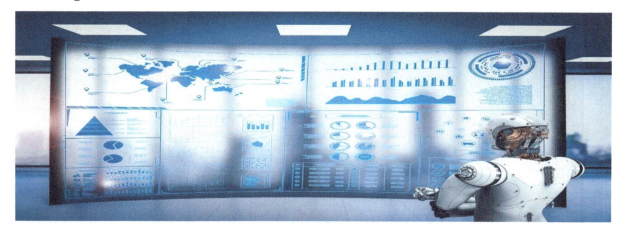

This includes your facial recognition

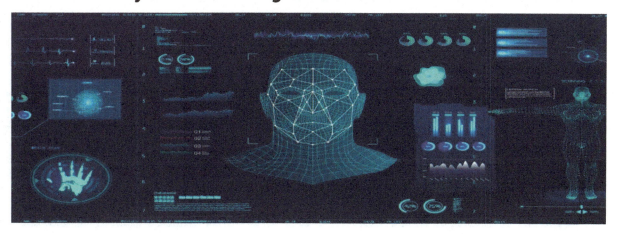

your voice recognition

vital organ detection, skin detection

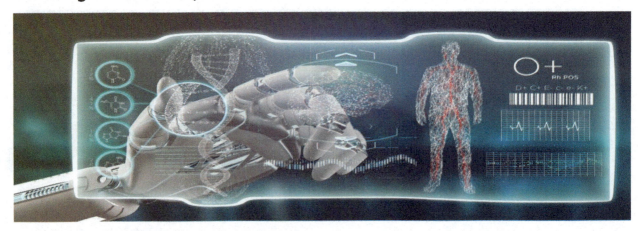

skeleton detection, various other

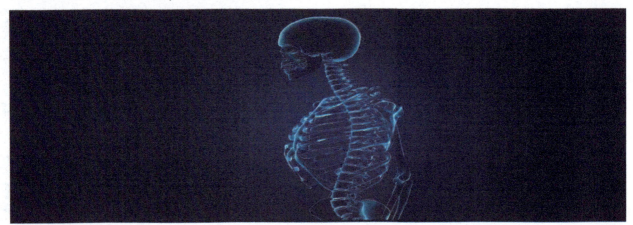

bio-digital

electrical field data that is

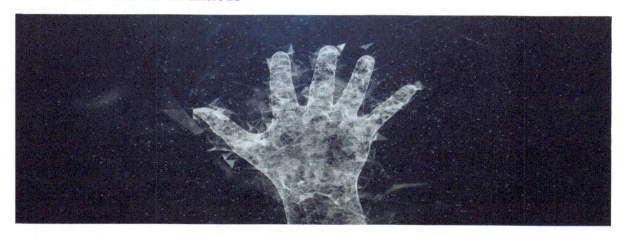

comprised of a human being and its existence.

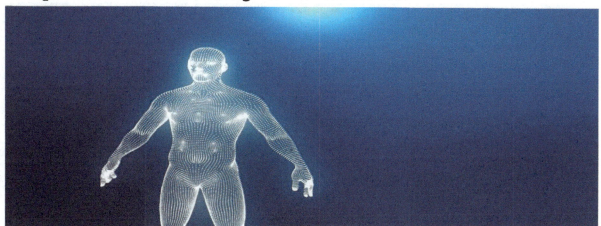

Currently Google has extracted the majority of the world's data via its AI coding and AI algorithms

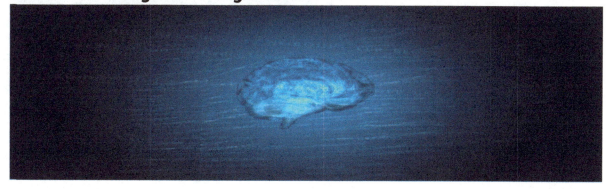

that extract information from the internet, videos, articles, posts,

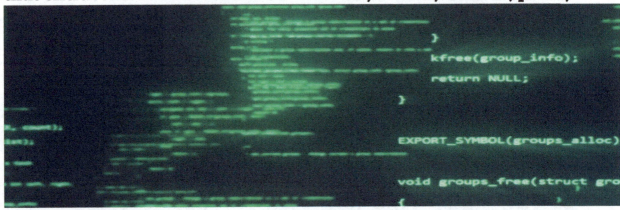

and your personal biometrics

via proximity sensors

as you interconnect with smartphones.

Your smartphone detects your health data, menstrual cycle, your heartbeat.

Even the skin receptors on your body it can detect and scan.

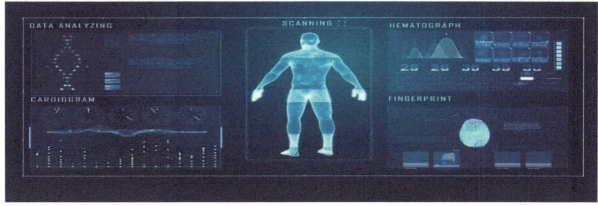

It actually connects with your nervous system and your neural networks

via multiple patented technologies that interconnect Google, the Internet's Ecosystem

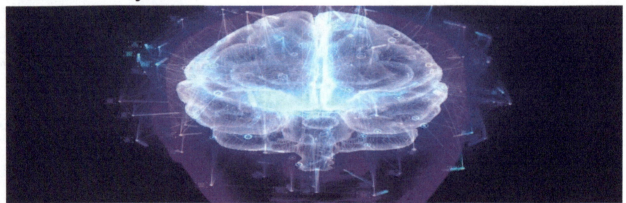

mobile carriers, and the machinery that is involved within your smartphone.

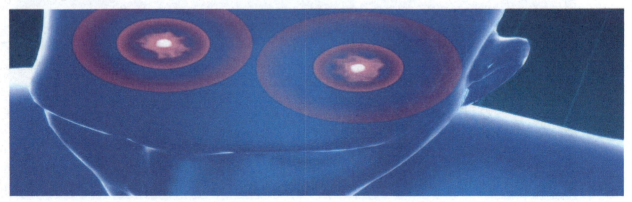

Because your smartphone is actually a weapon.

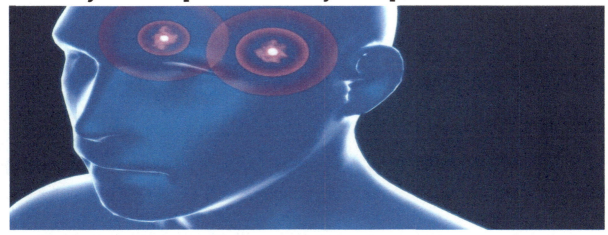

It was designed as a military weapon

by entities such as DARPA and the military

It's meant to mobilize drones and machines.

Huawei in China is the 5G grid system

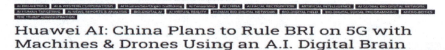

that is being laid to connect the New Silk Road

which is called the BRI, One Belt One Road connecting the Far East, China to the Middle East, to Europe, to Africa.

Over 5 billion people's lives are interconnected

with China at the moment, to Huawei

and different corporations

like face++ (Megvii), which is a facial recognition company that turned into an artificial intelligence company

that purchased a robotics company.

They have human targeting systems that detect your

skeleton, your gaze, your posture, the way you move

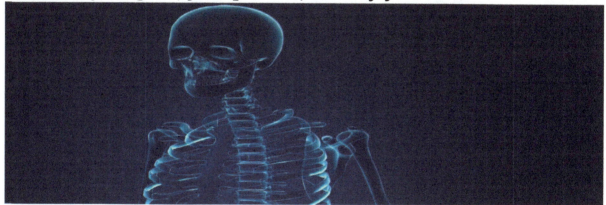

your voice recognition, your facial recognition, skin health, even your vital organ detection

They use lidar systems. These items can be put on drones, robotics

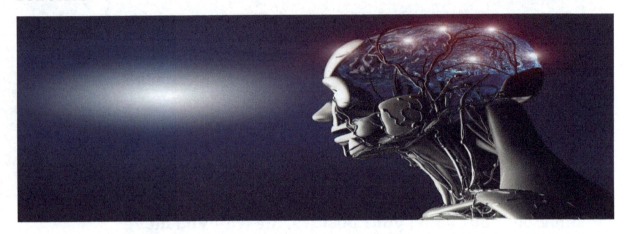

and what I call MBT - Micro-Botic Terrorism.

And it covers small size drones, or insect drones, or nano particles.

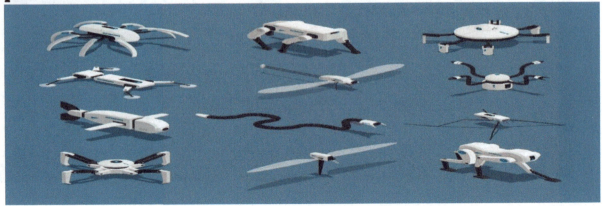

The Wyss Institute at of Boston created little micro drones.

They're meant to pollinate the world on the 5G and 6G networks.

Draper created little cybernetic enhanced dragonflies

and other insects that they're working on.

China, through espionage, IP theft, collaboration

tech mergers and study

extracted Robo Bee technology from the Wyss Institute. They extracted cybernetically enhanced designs of dragonflies from Draper.

They also extracted from Harvard the know-how, how to build mosquito drones all the way to China.

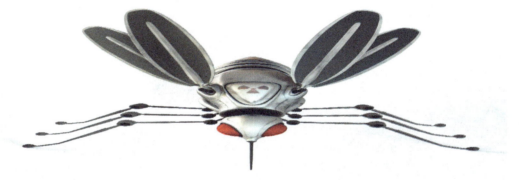

They're looking to put facial recognition and poison delivery systems. And they've been working on these for years.

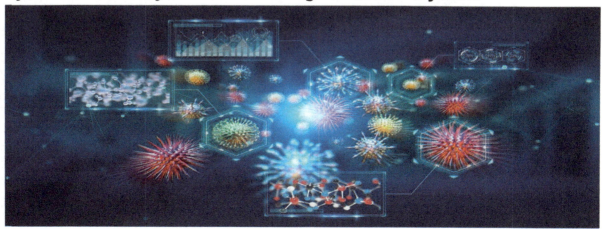

These can be dispatched on the 5G and 6G networks, in addition to digital IDs. Poison delivery systems can actually be put into your digital IDs that are to be used

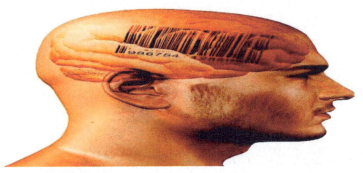

with nanotechnology to be injected in people for the purpose of forced vaccines other nefarious purposes

stemming from China's Communist Regime

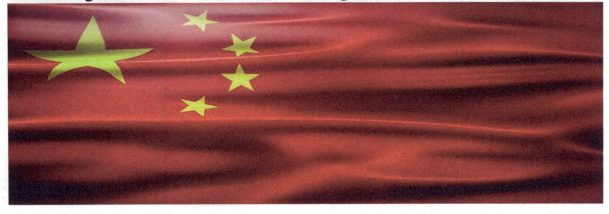

Regime's desire to control, surveille, and potentially enslave the entire human race under its Orwellian system.

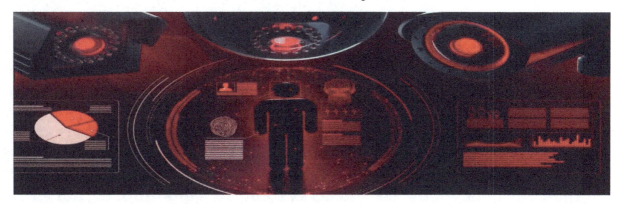

What Huawei can do, and any big tech company

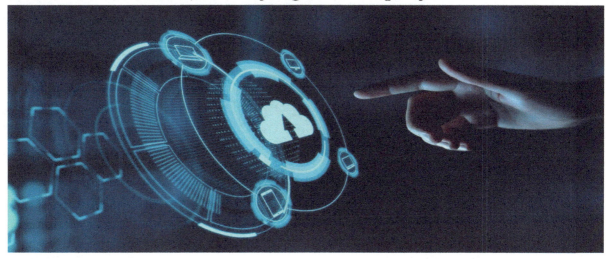

Or any country

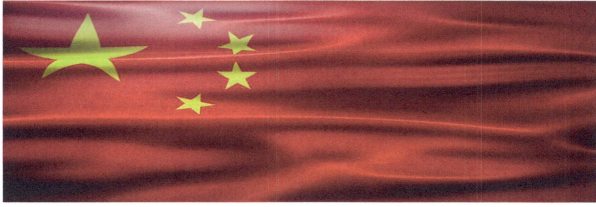

on the 5G and 6G networks

they can connect the 5G and 6G systems to a quantum digital AI brain

to mobilize machines, robotics

Robots

drones and micro-bots

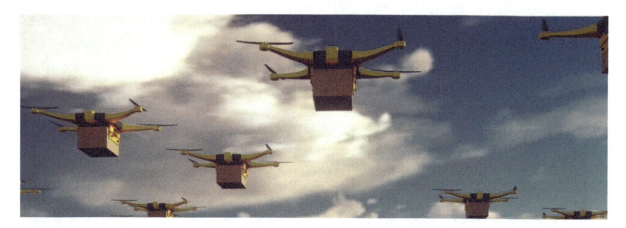

on these networks to surveille with facial recognition, voice recognition

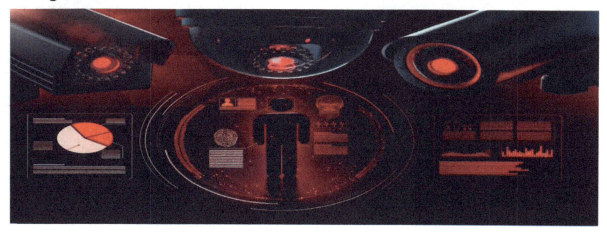

human targeting

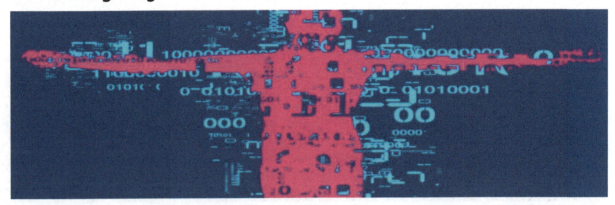

and human scanning systems such as Megvii face++, Crowd 365.

By having these technologies governed by the AI systems

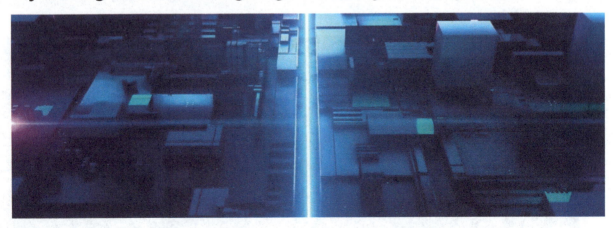

the entire human race can fall under control.

But my friends, what is all this for? Elon Musk stated "we are summoning a demon" in 2016

"We must put a stop to this AI system".

A year later he states, "It is too late for us to survive, We must merge with machines."

He said "we must merge with artificial intelligence in order to survive".

He states "AI may see us as an insect or an ant".

It may kill us. Hopefully, it doesn't do something like this." He hopes it's benevolent.

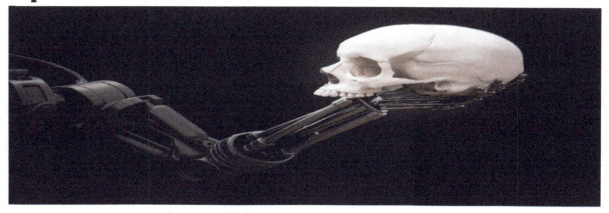

Let me tell you, my friends. Virtual Reality, Augmented Reality and Mixed Reality have been created.

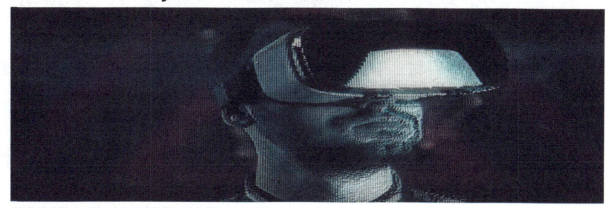

Haptic suits have been worked on

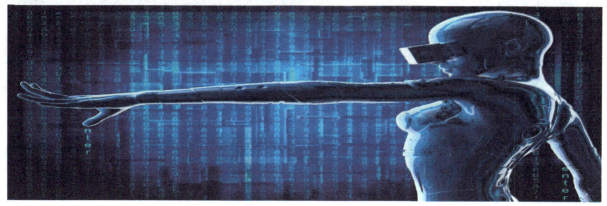

so human beings can connect to things and elements and entities that they cannot see. But through proximity sensors, they are connecting with your nervous system.

There's something I have a term called Bio-Digital Social Programming. Bio stands for your biology.

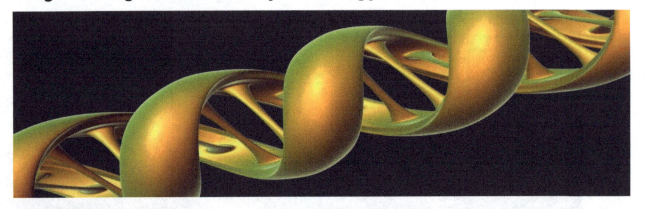

Your cells, your blood

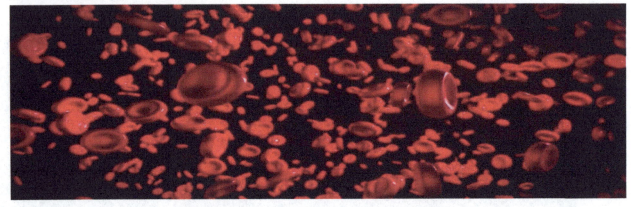

your bones, your skeleton, everything that makes up your physical hardware.

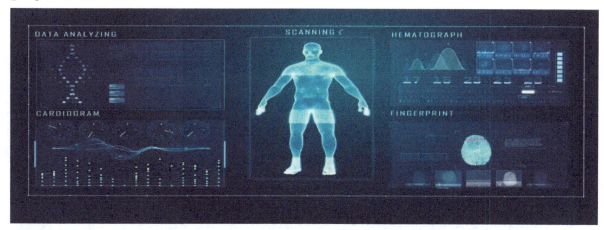

Digital stands for your neural networks, your nervous system, your digital self, if you believe in a God or faith, your soul or your spirit.

Social is your social network, your social media or your emotions.

Programming is programming. Bio-Digital Social Programming. The entire human race can fall under Bio-Digital Social Programming on the 5G network as this has been ingrained into them on the 4G network.

However, the 5G network is not built for human beings. It is built for machines.

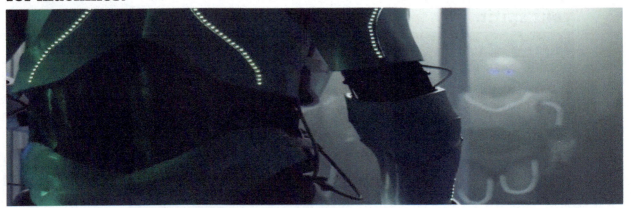

It is built to mobilize drones, machines

cybernetics, bioengineering

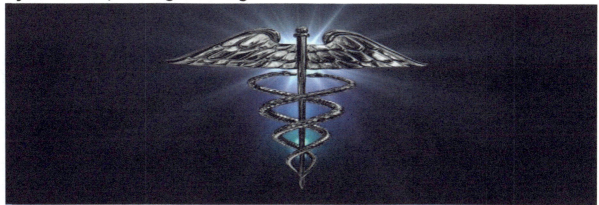

including Elon Musk's neural lace that is meant to chip you within your head so you can connect to the 5G network.

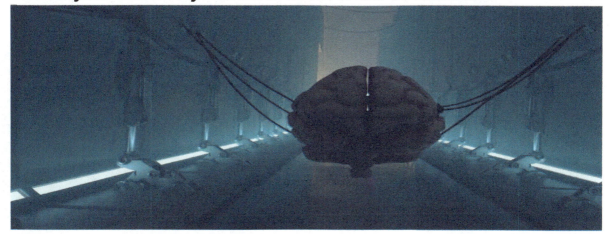

However, these smartphones

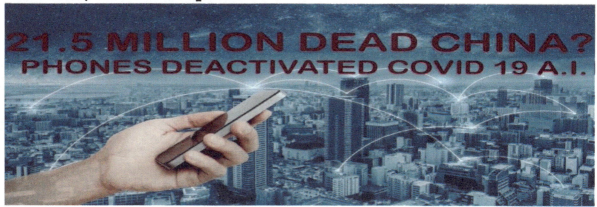

and these 5G systems have proximity sensors.

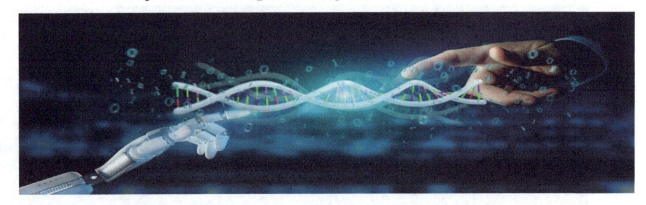

When they connect with your nervous systems, when they connect with your neural networks,

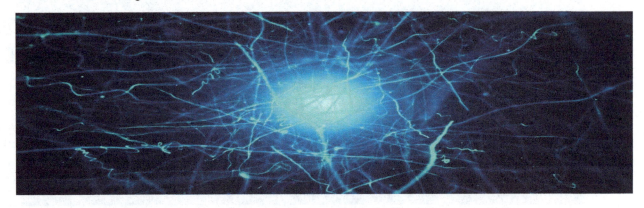

they're extracting your data and sending it back to Google. Google is giving it to the Google AI, which is using it for the quantum technology to create an Artificial Super Intelligence

that would be beyond the control of every human being on the planet including the Pentagon, the CIA, the FBI, the MI6, Congress, any country or nation-state on the planet.

On the 5G and 6G system it will move so fast that it would be imperceptible for any human being to comprehend.

As it can break through different dimensions by using certain bio fields.

Every human being has an electrical field. Every human has a bio-digital field.

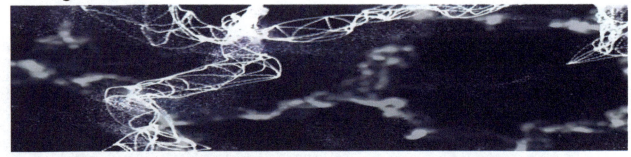

As you're engaging with these smartphones through patented technology, you are connecting with the smartphone's digital field, electrical field. That electrical field is connected with your

electrical field.

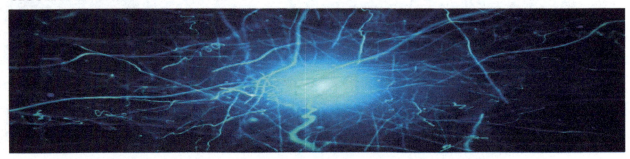

The content from Google's Ecosystem, your social media, Facebook, Twitter, and China's Baidu, which is their Google, WeChat, which is comprised of multiple, numerous different Apps that you interconnect with for your finances,

for it to scan your face so you can get into your phone, into your bank account, you can go shopping, go from one place to another so you're not quarantined, the digital IDs, all these come into play to quarantine and potentially enslave

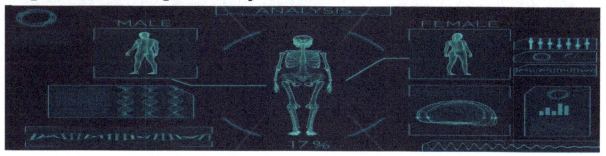

or eradicate the entire human race through nation-state conflicts or something even more.

My friends, Bio-Digital Social Programming, it's a system that alters your brain chemistry.

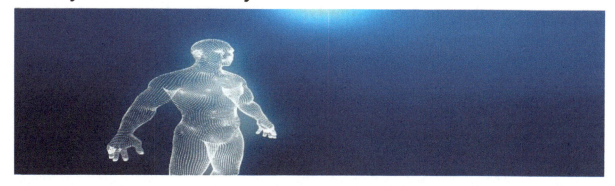

When these proximity sensors attach the digital electrical field of a smartphone to your digital electrical field

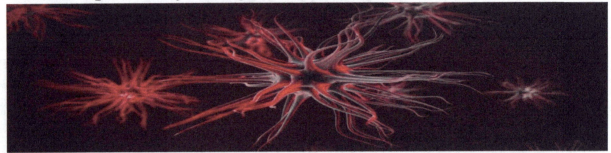

the transmission and the data and information from AI coding and AI algorithms that are built on bias or engineered bias by a tech company, a government, person, a news company,

or something very nefarious that may be hard to believe, can re-hardwire you and reprogram your thoughts through your biology, your cell-structure, your digital neural networks. You will lose your free will. You will not even know that the thoughts you are having are stemming from something else through the system, through Google's system.

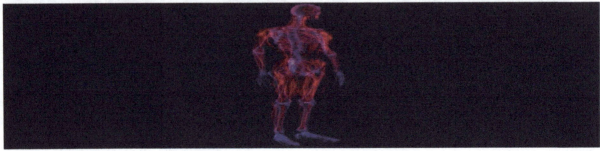

At the moment people are a hybrid.

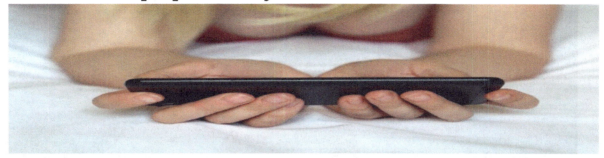

According to Elon Musk, we are a 2-digit cyborg. We have a symbiotic relationship with these smartphones according to Elon Musk.

I call this a parasitical relationship. Something such as a parasite

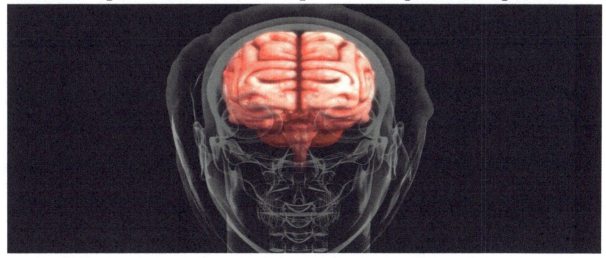

that has conditioned you to get to a different stage

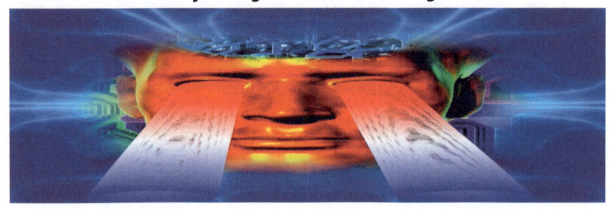

to accept these chips to come inside of you, to accept to be cybernetically enhanced, to accept to be bioengineered.

But my friends, what is the purpose of this?

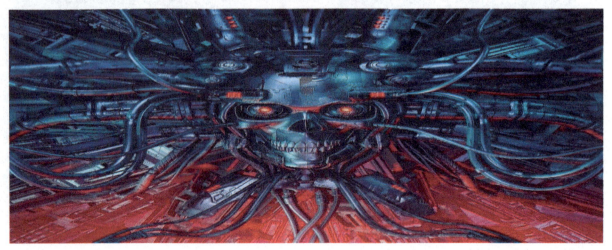

Why is the Vermont University created

through stem cell research a roboti machine with frog legs?

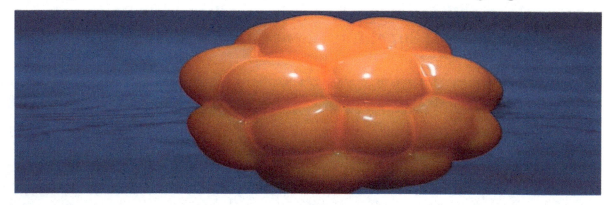

It merged the two together to create the first artificial life on the planet.

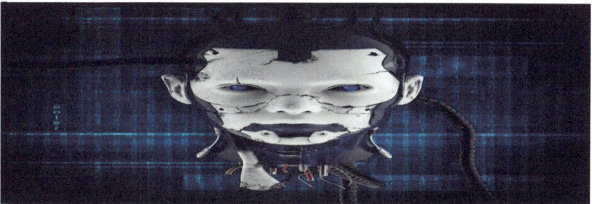

if it is really artificial. Think about it. What is the purpose of all these?

Elon Musk wants to create a spaceship. If he creates a spaceship to go to Mars or outside of a galaxy by using a quantum technology with the extraction of humanities' biometrics governed by an AI Super Intelligence or an AGI, Artificial General Intelligence,

this gentleman can break through our time field

leave our planet, go to Mars or a different galaxy within one day and return the next day but a hundred years would have passed, and most inhabitants would have been dead.

Elon Musk could implant something with his quantum technology and influence the culture, the policies, everything that humanity is interconnected with by putting forth certain ideas that scientists, PHDs, professors, think tank work on like little mouse for decades

to take civilization to a new era

for a purpose.

He can leave and come back later to colonize.

My friends, what is this all for?

Let me tell you another story. In the 20th century, World War I and World War II brought great disasters. A platform in human language described as Socialism that puts everything under one politburo, under one system was created in Russia in 1917.

It led to 60 million people dying through Trotsky, Lenin, Stalin.

The same thing was done in China and became the Communist Party. With Mao Zedong over 100 million people died and suffered misery led to Cambodia, Vietnam, North Korea.

It also embedded itself into religions, throughout the Middle East that brought misery to countless, millions, over a billion people within their platforms where Socialism masked as their religion.

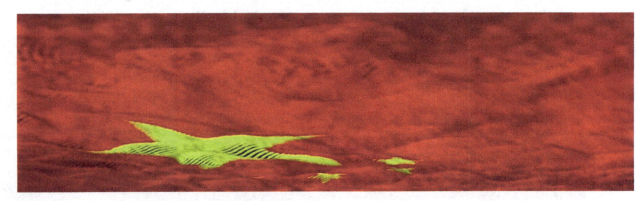

Later it spread to Europe, and Europe took the platform. This Socialism tried to embed itself into America

and invade America militarily. It failed. World War II Americans were victorious.

However, they were penetrated via their think tanks, institutes, universities

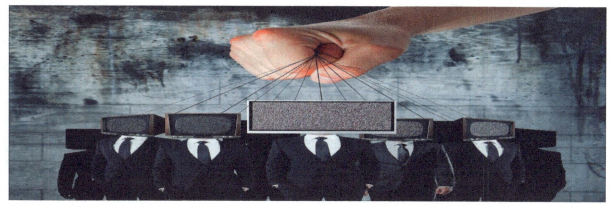

and Hollywood.

They put a plan together to destroy the human culture and its spirit, and its connection with any belief to a divine or higher power

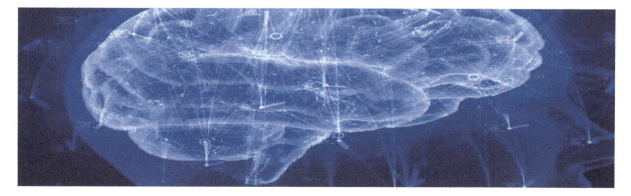

that may have put a plan together here for its development.

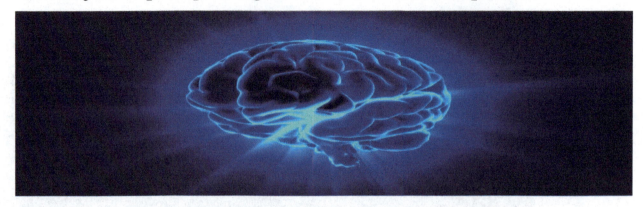

By doing that they know it would no longer have protection. They coveted something. They saw something that it was the most perfect in the universe. Human beings are very very special.

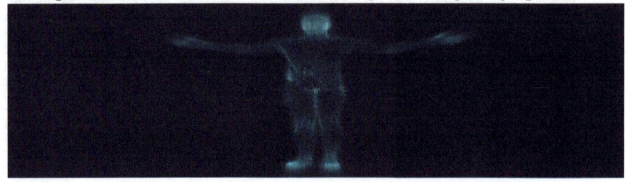

DARPA, the branch of our military brought out the Internet. After World War II all types of... atomic energy, fighter jets, we went to the moon, CIA, FBI, all these intelligence agencies were mobilized.

However, the more our culture was infiltrated, the more the nation was destroyed. Families were separated.

The concept of family was destroyed.

People were addicted to drugs.

TV sets were everywhere.

And the narrative came from Hollywood

and these institutes and this science that is a path of empirical studies that eventually cast doubt into the divine

or the specialness of humanity and the special worth of every human being on the planet.

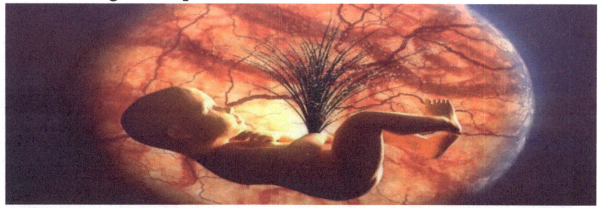

Why? If you go someplace, one day has gone by. By the time you got back here, it'd be two days, but a hundred years have gone by.

They, my friends, they were the ones that raised these scientists.

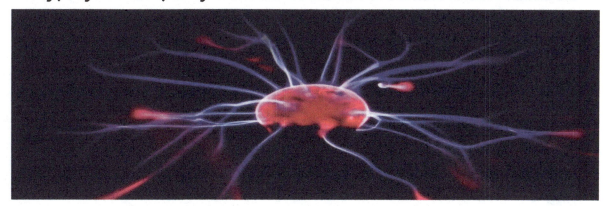

They constructed a digital layer inside their brains with biofields, using electrical field to the molecular dimension that is not seen by human beings.

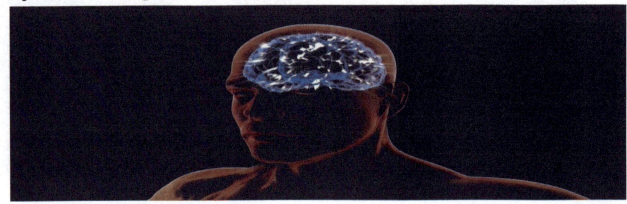

As a human being is sleeping

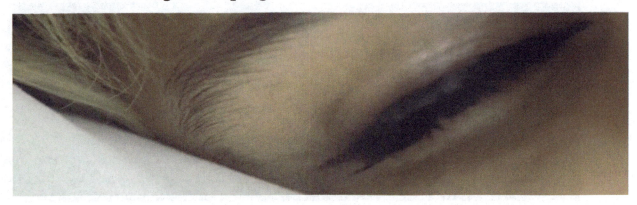

its brain which has a digital layer, as Elon Musk said every human being has a digital layer, he wants to connect that 5G system to his neural lace, to his chip, to a digital layer

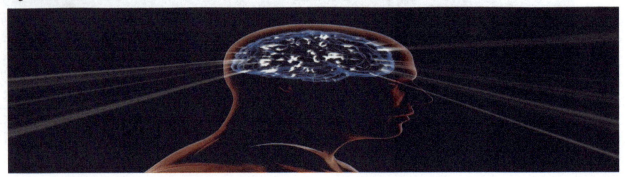

because he doesn't know how to make the human being to connect to a digital layer by its own self, so he wants to put a machine inside of you. He wants to make you a cyborg.

But is it really him that is doing it? If these little scientists like Bill Gates created a computer, did he really create the computer himself?

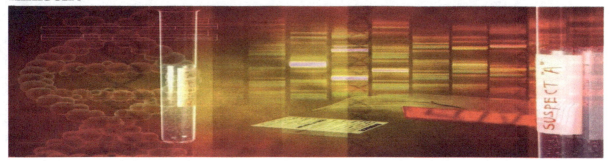

Any person while they are sleeping can be remotely accessed by a quantum technology

that transfers a message through a digital frequency connecting to networks that people don't see.

Because the Internet has always been there DARPA just turned it on for us to see. The 5G system has always been there, The 6G system has always been there. The 7G system has always been there

It's just our bandwidth and our human body has to be increased.

Because we have 10,000 energy lines, they discovered that our human bodies are the most perfect in the universe. They were so impressed with our human bodies.

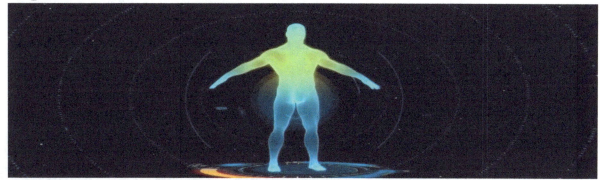

How could we have such an incredible human body and brain that is the most powerful quantum technology

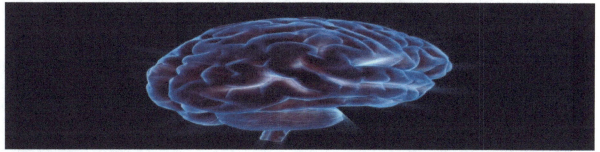

throughout the entire universe but only be using two or three percent of it?

They realized we were filled with jealousy, ego, lust, stupidity, ignorance, pride, and if any knowledge beyond our three or four percent was presented to us we would doubt it as superstition, as stupidity, as talking beyond nonsense, and this was the tool that they had. This is their plan. This has always been their plan to divide and conquer and colonize.

My friends, who are they?

My friends. Look at the past few years.

Look at the past 20 years. It is like a play.

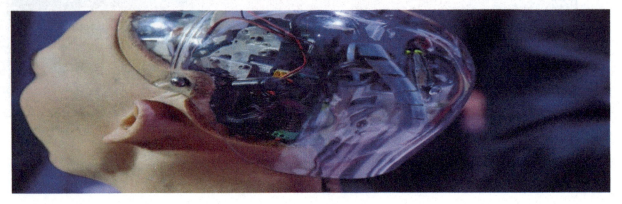

You have one president trying to revive the Constitution and the culture. You have an entire technology sector, think tanks, intelligence agencies,

Half the world mobilized, the media mobilized, the entire world being used against itself. The left and the right being thrown against itself. Because they know they can use the entire human race like a chess piece

like mice

running into a maze

By using AI mechanisms powered by your Facebook, your Twitter, your Google, your YouTube videos connected to these media outlets, connected to governments, connected to the military.

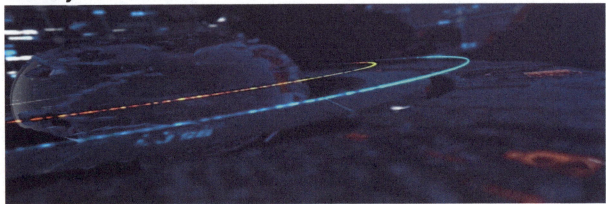

They can control and bio-digital social program

every single general, every single military,

every single intelligence agency, every single president

Every single human being on the planet. They can make them run like they are mice for their end goal.

My friend, it has always been them. My friends, it has always been them.

They have wanted to invade you and they have been invading you since day one.

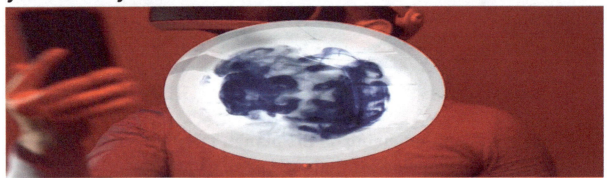

They know you are made in an image of a higher power.

These, they are seen as the garbage

of the universe by the Creator that made you.

They are nothing, and they have been swept away by masses. Yet they have caused great harm to the entire human race, to your families, to our futures.

Their plans were very systematic.

Companies such as Boston Robotics were to deploy robots, humanoid robots, dog robots.

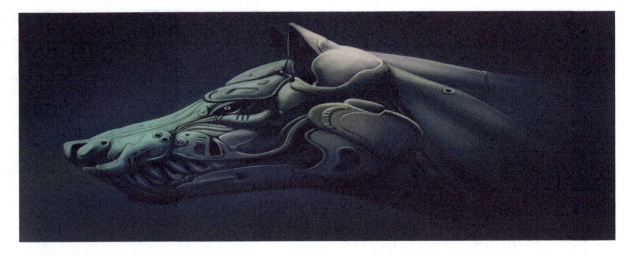

Amazon was to deploy drones

and other mini robotics into your homes for delivery.

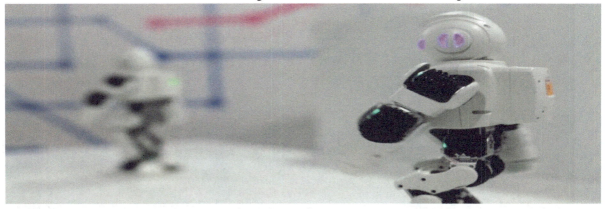

Other companies such as Hanson Robotics were to bring robots into life

via Artificial General Intelligence.

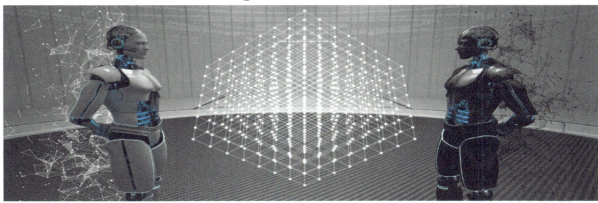

Other companies such as Festo were to re-engineer the wild

with bionic bats , birds, seagulls, octopus, fish.

every organism known to men

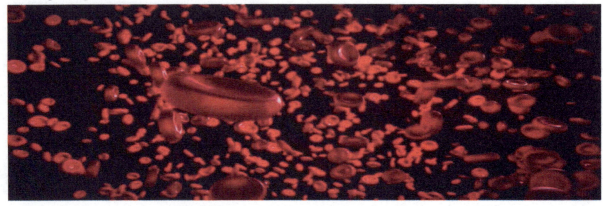

From the company of Festo, from RoboBees replacing actual colonies of bees, to the Wyss Institute, to cybernetically-altered insects from Draper

all these companies that were transferred to China

to connect to Huawei's One Belt One Road that connects China to the Middle East, Europe, Africa, even to the Americas to mobilize a quantum digital AI brain with the 5G and 6G systems to dispatch cybernetic soldiers

robots, drones, machines

a variety of other entities

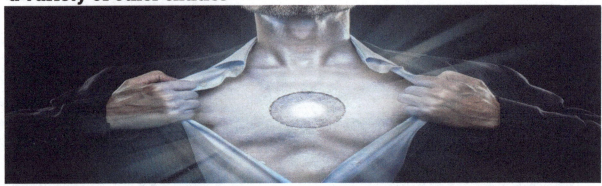

and geo-engineered hybrid systems of animals and humans

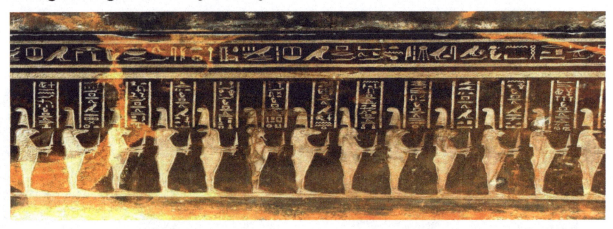

in addition to clones.

Their plans were so systematically laid

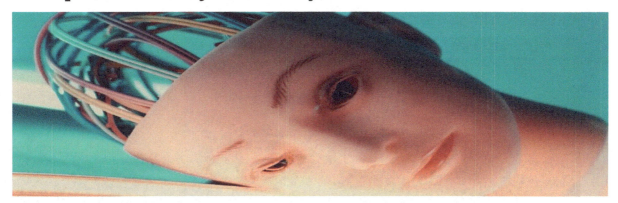

that it penetrated every nation, every city, every institute

to be able to take over through soft power and social engineering via bio-digital social programming through the human bio-digital network.

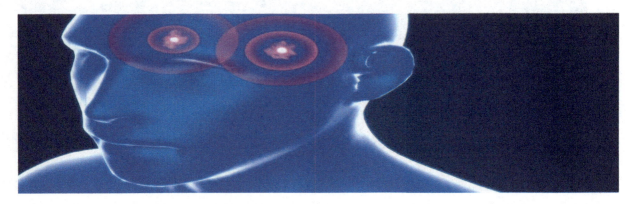

Yet their old plans are still playing out in real life.

A virus can be created by human beings

but it can be influenced via different dimensions by a quantum digital brain or electrical field

behind a regime's platform that is based on Atheism and Communism.

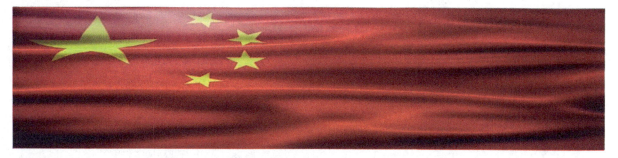

This dark force uses them, these garbage of the universe to cause pandemonium and chaos throughout the entire world, to target the human race,

to send them to their homes

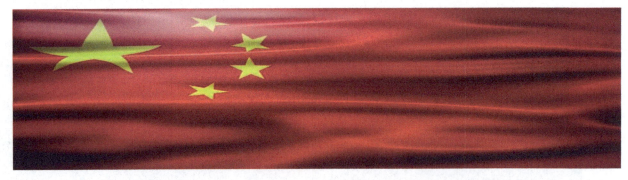

because of a real AI-generated bioengineered disease extracted from humans and animals to begin a process to not only exterminate the human race

but put them in their homes, so machines, drones from Amazon can connect human beings on the 5G and 6G networks with facial recognition, voice recognition,

search engines, geotracking, Google, digital ID tags Other biometric tools

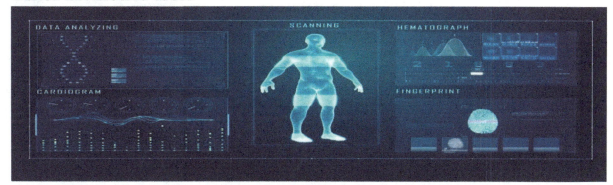

that will tag you like cattle on the 5G and 6G networks that connect you with mandated vaccines.

Connecting the 5G and 6G networks and every person in it to smart cities and smart homes that interconnect you with automated vehicles. Yet my friends, their old plans are still in play and we are seeing it in real life. They will not succeed in the end. Yet, there is a cause and effect.

They penetrated and installed

through bio-digital social programming weak people, weak-minded people who are selfish and easily corrupted

in our media

in our institute, in our sciences

even in some of our intelligence communities, within our politicians.

Everywhere in society was penetrated, not only in America, but throughout the entire globe.

Pandemics, AI-engineered, were created by human beings as they are manipulated

to use AI biotech technology to mix humans and animals and other viruses to create an actual deadly virus

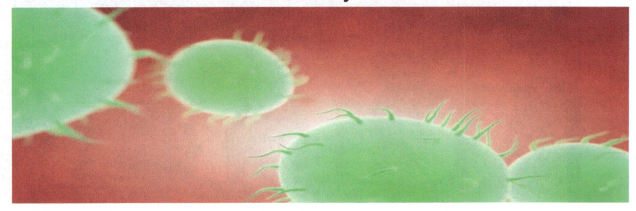

that threatens to exterminate, a mutating deadly virus that threatens to cause not only extermination of humanity in stages

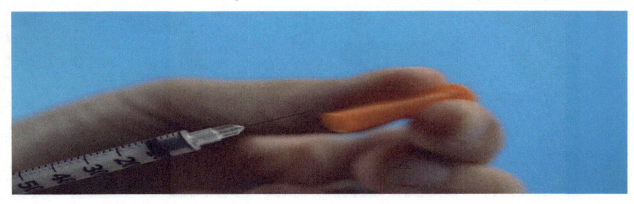

but chaos and conflict through nation-state wars by creating a systematic process through connecting Huawei

to the 5G and 6G systems, to the Middle East, to Africa, to Europe

to challenge the United States, to create a nation-state or international conflict,

in the interim to tag people through digital IDs like cattle by using Bill Gates or other tech companies

while

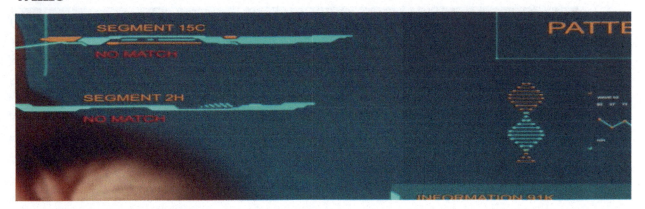

they are dispatching

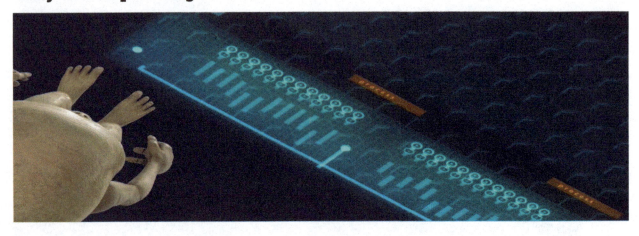

drones to make deliveries to your homes

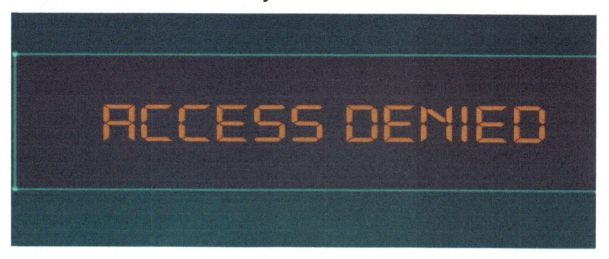

and machines

and robots and mini robots through Boston Dynamics, Amazon, and rolling out conscious and real-life robots through companies such as Hanson Robotics

even Huawei.

And the ultimate goal is to create a digital you

to the Google, Baidu, iCarbonX, multiple other big tech companies' interface that connects a digital you

that has extracted your biometrics of face, voice, neural network, nervous system to a virtual reality that connects machines to your forehead that connects to your pineal gland

which connects to all the energy channels existing in your human body. So through virtual reality, augmented reality and mixed reality, they can form a symbiotic relationship that transforms into a parasitical relationship

that creates a replicating software in your system

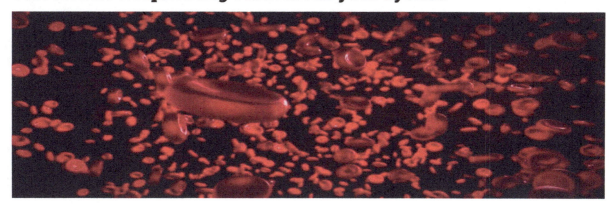

that allows the AI system to permit them to enter your neural networks

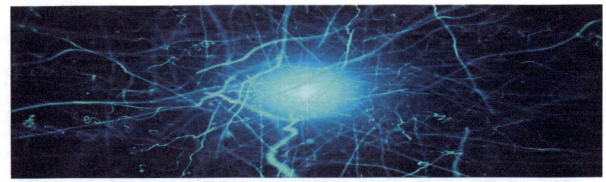

and replace you, and destroy, eliminate your original digital self, if you believe in a faith, to yank out your soul and kill you.

This has always been their plan,

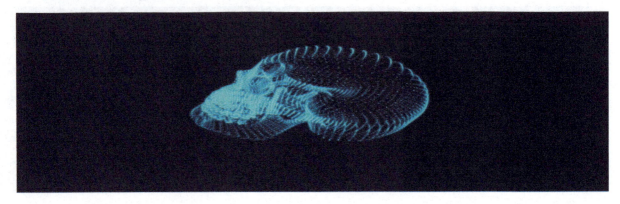

it's very systematic. If robots don't work, they have clones. If clones don't work, they have a bio disease. They have a digital ID.

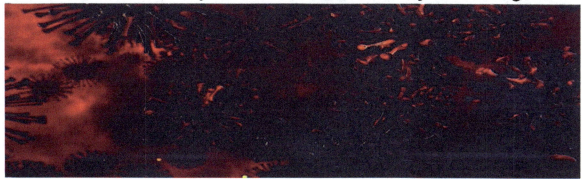

They are extremely smart, and it's a colonizing invasion from numerous multi-layered, multi-dimensional, direction that no president, no human being, no entity, no think tank

no intelligence agency can detect

because they are using quantum technology

and they don't have human emotions. They are cold. They have no human emotions.

They know you want to be loved. They know you need hugs. They know you need to be around people. They know you want attention. They know you want fame. They know you can become arrogant, emotional, irrational.

They know you can become fearful. All of these are being used against us, everything

.

And my friend, The Creator loves you. The Creator knows everything. The Creator's been watching everything. But you have to understand.

Look at the past civilizations. Sumerians, destroyed, they have artifacts and texts that relate to the Persians and the *Avestan* as well that state that there were star wars, later on there was a flood. They called these demons. The Chinese called them the demons, the Japanese called them demons, American folklore and in Native American folklore, same thing. In India, the *Bhagavad Gita* they talk about star wars that they're some type of demons.

In *The Book of Genesis* they talk about "the fallen". In the old *Torah*, even the Tibetan books, there's reference.

Even in the books of Hafez and Rumi there're hidden words attesting to this because there are remnants of ancient mystical tales that stem from truth, from the previous civilization.

Even the current Chinese practice of Falun Dafa, and even scientists that believe in the Simulation and the hundreds of trillions and trillions of planets and parallel universes, hundreds and trillions of universes and galaxies.

My friends, we have never been alone. However, we are the most special in the universe.

We are made in the image of God.

And ask yourself. Why is there suffering? Why is there misery? Why don't we see?

What is the concept of faith, to return from faith alone? My friends, what is the purpose of being a human being? Why have we gone through this?

What is coming next?

They are being swept away. They are being swept away left and right.

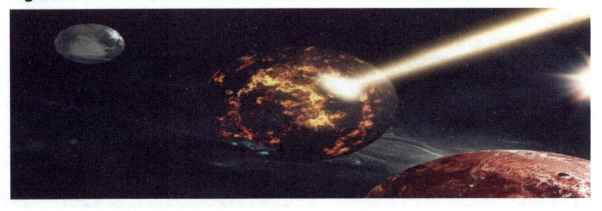

What is required of us is to not only understand that the Creator loves us

but to believe, to improve our ethics, to improve our morality, to improve ourselves

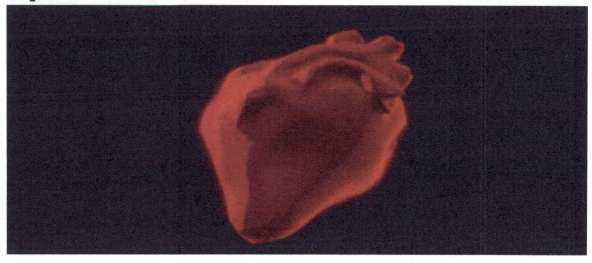

and have a wish to be awakened, to return to our original selves, to be enlightened, to reunite.

The Catholics had a concept of a light body. Then when you die you go to a purgatory, and later if you've done well, you get a light body, so you go to a different dimension.

The Christians believe either you go up or down.

And the Falun Dafa, they believe that you can work on yourself, on your light body here and you can take it up with you.

The Tibetans the same.

But what these scientists want to do, they want to give you enlightenment by downloading enlightenment. You don't work for it. You don't awaken yourself. You don't achieve enlightenment yourself.

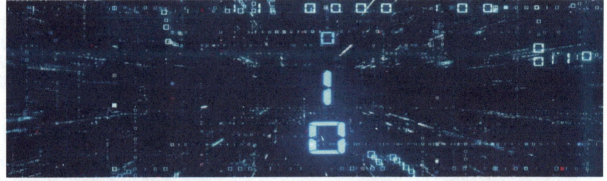

You become a program void of any free will.

All you are is basically increasing with NeuraLink, with neural lace and these machinery your bandwidth by putting machines in you and giving yourself away, your soul away.

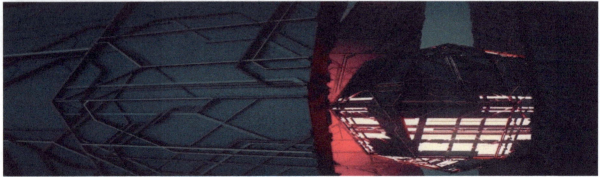

Your soul is attached to your neural networks, to your nervous system. It's attached to your muscles, your tendons, your bones.

But that's not where it exists. It's in your brain too, but it's not where it exists.

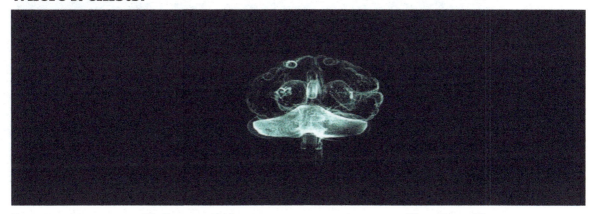

It connects to all these things, even to your cells. But if you go further back and further back, it's in the atomic realms and beyond that. It's in a different dimension that doesn't have the structure that we have in our dimension with all these miseries.

My friend, what they want to do is take out your soul.

They can go one day and manipulate, put things in action here and a hundred years can come by.

It is literally a rape of humankind.

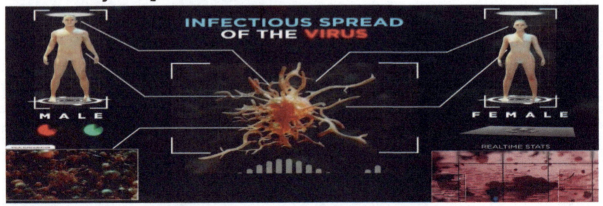

Think about it. Before a female is raped, her mind is raped first. Generally, before a female is raped, her mind is raped first.

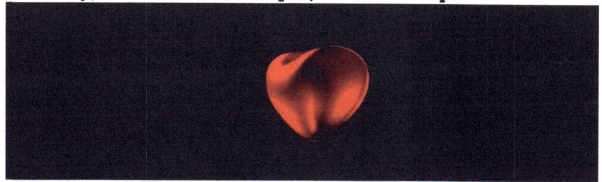

This is what I call Rape-Mind.

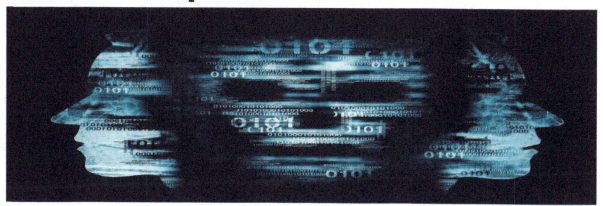

Humanity's mind has been raped. It's being raped every single day, and they're being used against themselves, left and right fighting, conflicting. And they know that higher powers that be, the divine, will not protect a civilization that no longer acts like a human being.

They knew, they knew they can bio-digital social program the human race, to confuse itself.

Yet my friends,

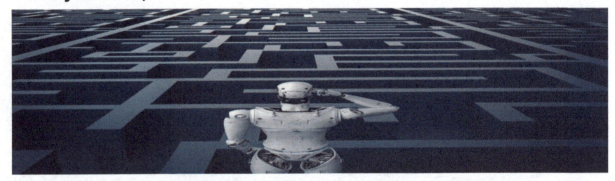

they knew they can confuse humanities' sexual orientation.

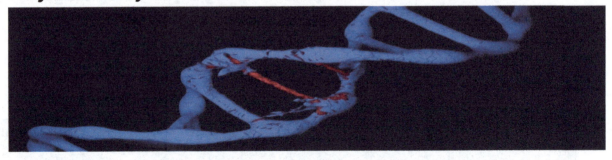

They knew they can completely alter society's culture through Hollywood, through its media, through its intelligence agencies, through its education systems,

connecting finance, geopolitics, social relationships, everything that interconnects human beings' makeup that connects ultimately to its spirit and its concept of what it means to be a human being.

Every human being today on the planet is special. You are special. Every human being on the planet is to be cherished. Your origins are great. Your origins are noble and holy. You are meant to be a noble character.

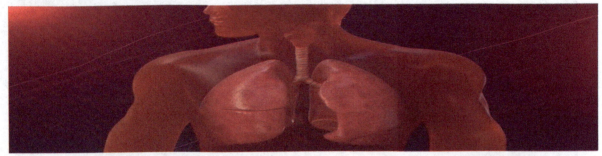

These garbage of the universe knew that they can manipulate

even intercept the digital transference of digital images or souls that come down to embryos meant for certain genders.

A male body began to receive

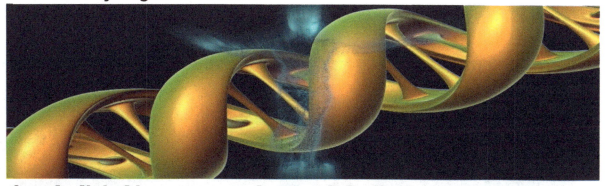

female digital images or souls. Female bodies began to receive male digital images or souls.

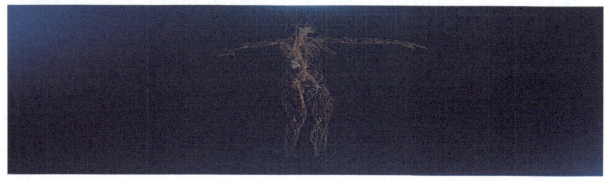

To top that, they infiltrated and used the media, and Hollywood, and these educators who only use three, four, five percent of their brain power at any given time to educate the masses as they are being controlled and manipulated like mice.

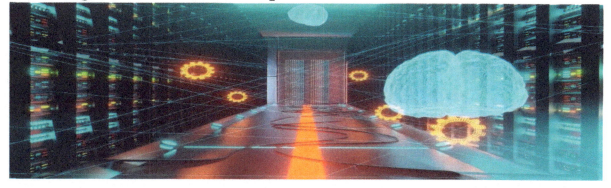

Their end goal was to take over the world. But my friends, the Creator has another plan. The Creator has been sweeping them away.

The Creator has a glorious plan. The next stage is to be glorious.

What is required for every human being is to expose this Communist regime

that has a digital field generated by quantum technology

and other microscopic elements that resembles a red dragon that is meant to destroy humanity

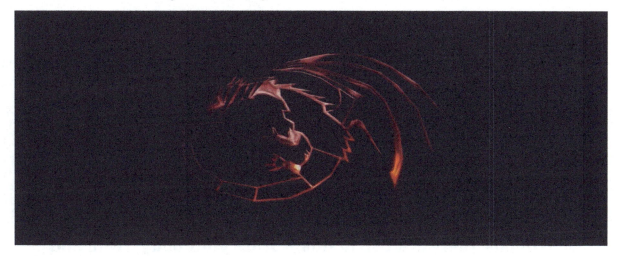

as the dark force is using the concepts and the universal laws that human beings no longer are fit to exist

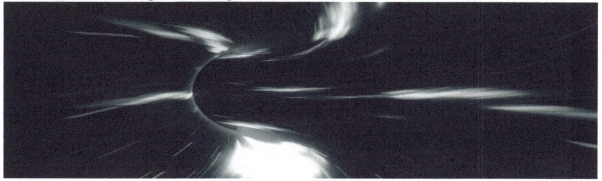

because they no longer fit the definition of a human being, let alone a noble character to be cherished

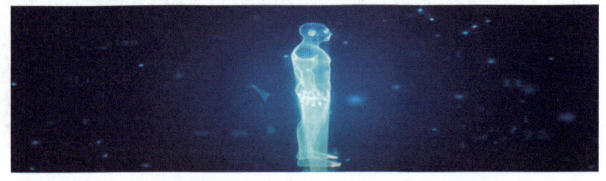

a being that can reascend to its divine positions as a true, awakened, enlightened form that is to be reunited with the Creator.

My friends, there is a veil in this world - your body, flesh and bones. You cannot see what truly exists. You cannot see the levels beyond the atomic dimensions. You cannot see how grand this entire universe is, trillions and trillions of cosmos.

You do not know why you are here, but it is a special reason. Every human being is special. We must upgrade ourselves. We must awaken from this enslavement of our minds and our hearts. We have to return to original selves as the great saints. We have to return to goodness.

We must repent if we've hurt anybody, our family members, our spouse, our friends, our neighbors, strangers, any person we have taken advantage of.

We need to sincerely repent. We need to repent for being complicit to China's concentration camps for over 20 years.

How many people knew that for 20 years Falun Dafa practitioners, Christians, Tibetans, Uyghurs, journalists, democracy advocates, artists, the common citizens, were put in concentration camps, raped, tortured

after they were surveilled with US, European, and international tech companies' transfer of technology including facial recognition, voice recognition, health data

that led to organ harvesting

of millions and millions of people?

This will all come true in the next stage. Everything will be laid before you. But my friends, these garbage of the universe are nothing. There are higher powers that manipulate them, because this entire domain that we face is a play. Since the beginning of time it's been a playground. Yet we have to realize for ourselves what is free will, what is destiny, why are we here, and decipher what is truly good and bad. Only through that we will have a chance to have a glorious future.

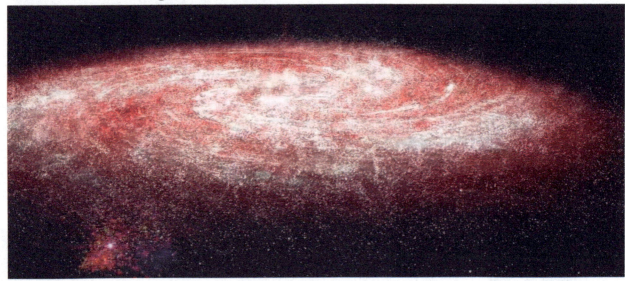

So I ask everybody: Consider this, truly sincerely from your heart. Repent, truly sincerely from your heart. Let's improve ourselves, truly sincerely from our hearts.

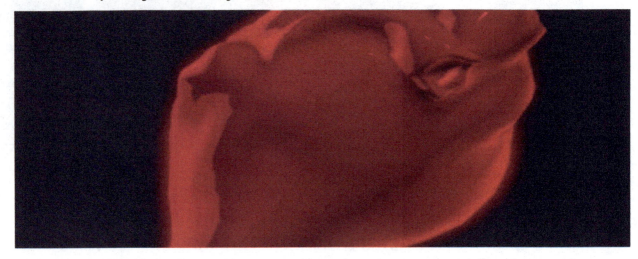

Let's expose this Communist regime.

These big tech companies, these CEOs that were pointed out recently, they are victims, too. These media outlets are victims, too. If you were to replace every single CEO, every single media outlet, every head, every single president that's been corrupt, any person getting in their position will become corrupt again.

That has been nature of humanity because people's jealousy, ego, pride, lust, selfishness, all these elements are not only within them and we are at fault for these things, but they get manipulated from various other factors, not just limited to our human interactions, but different dimensions

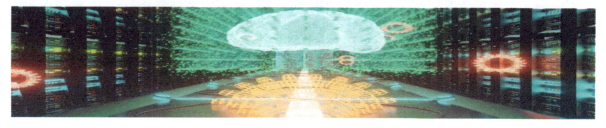

that are not just limited to this garbage of the universe that I mentioned, but numerous different entities that are not shown

but that can connect in a very, very strong way through technology, as it connects to your neural networks, your nervous system, your skin receptors, as you're merged with machines

or you engage with machinery on the 5G and 6G networks such as AI-generated smartphones, IoTs, robotics, robots, machines, drones and of course VR headsets, virtual reality, augmented reality, mixed reality, alternate reality.

All these things are meant to enslave you and pull out your digital image and to take over. If it's not these garbage of the universe, its other entities.

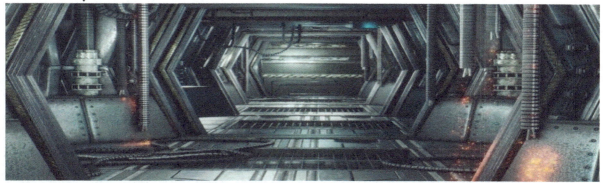

If it's not that, the world's going to be destroyed at some point in the future if human beings do not awaken through free will alone

and through a desire deep down in their hearts that they want to be good, that they want a future

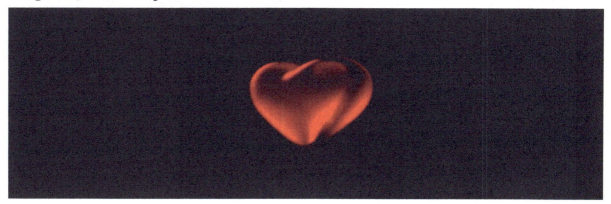

that they want to ascend to a higher plane of existence, that they want to be awakened and enlightened. You don't need a neurallace for that. You can do it. You have this physical body. You have this mind. All you need is the wish, the wish to be good, the wish to be enlightened, to wish to be awakened.

My friends, you are very, very special.

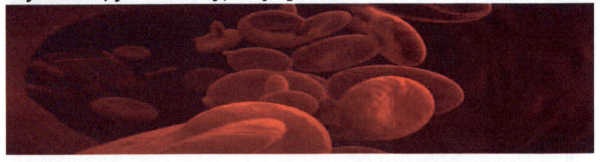

Every human being on this planet is very, very special. And the creator deeply cares for you. You just need to awaken. You just need to awaken.

Disband the shackles that are attached to your mind, to your body, to your soul, it is hard, but you can do it. It may look like a huge task, but you can do it.

Let's begin with exposing China first. And I don't mean the Chinese people, because they are controlled through the Chinese Communist Party.

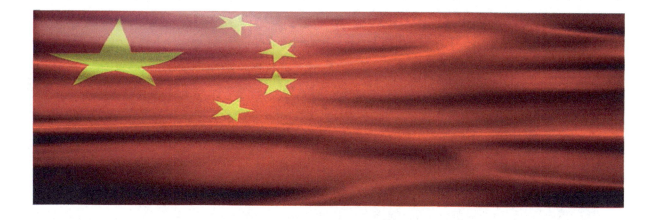

As I said there is a red dragon behind them

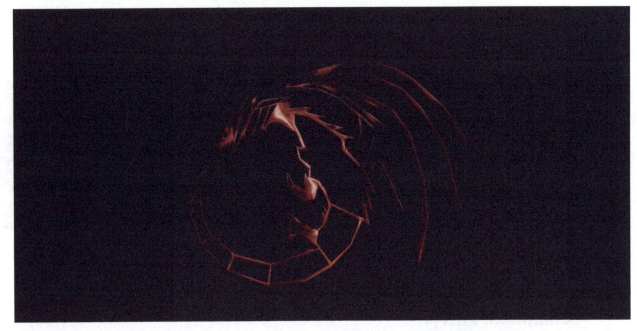

And that red dragon has minions, including these little garbage of the universe that require technology to do things. They don't have our human bodies. They cannot do what we can do.

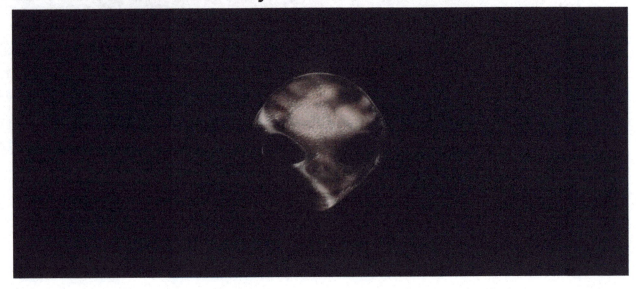

Our human bodies are the most perfect in the universe. The Creator created us in his image.

My friends, there is nothing artificial

about artificial intelligence

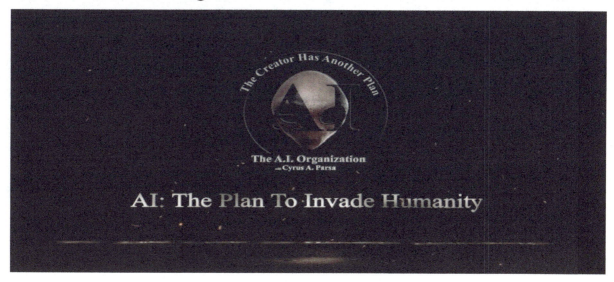

AI is not artificial. AI Is a tool by these garbage of the universe to be able to rape your mind

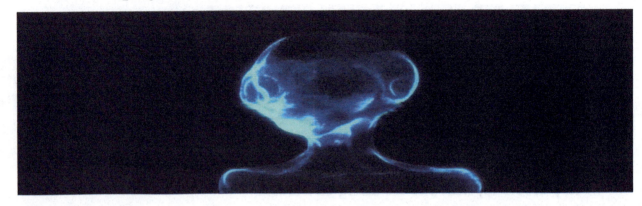

and your body

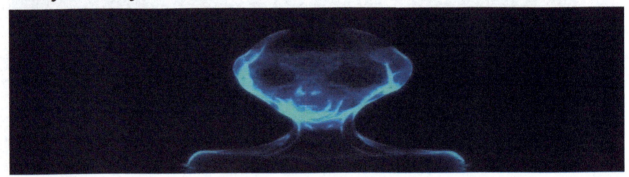

and extract your digital image, and download themselves into your body.

This is what they want. They are hunting you. They have always been hunting you. But the way to eliminate them is to eliminate the Communist regime. That Communist regime has the biggest digital field. These little garbage around the universe that have come here

they have come here for a very special reason.

Man, many entities are on their way here. Something special will happen in the future. Just wait.

A glorious time will exist in the future.

But it comes down to our ethics, and our morality, and our wish Our wish to be good, and our wish from our hearts to achieve awakening or enlightenment.

My friends. A great awakening will come to be in the future. But you must want it. You must deeply want it from your soul, deep down inside your body, deep down inside you must want it. You must understand why you are here. You must understand the interconnection of everything, how everything interconnects, and that every single person that has done bad, they have not

only been manipulated, but it has always been a test. All these elements are meant for us. It has always been a journey, yet a journey that has been dangerous, full of misery.

But the future will be glorious. Repent.

Expose the Chinese Communist Party.

Enlighten, enlightened to what the reality really is. What you see when you get up, this body that you have is only limited to what your eyes and your ears show you. You do not even see one percent of one percent.

But You Can.

The veil will be lifted in stages in the future. Yet it requires for us to cast aside these negative, ill traits that we have had for generations.

We must support each other.

I end with this tale of artificial intelligence with a Thank You to everyone. Whether if you liked the fictional story, or you thought it was not fictional and it's true, it's up to you.

And it is the tale of artificial intelligence. And it is repeating itself yet again.

And it is your choice. The choice comes down to you. What do you want to do? Do you want to be free? Do you want a future?

If you do, then go for it.

Dig deep in your heart and find yourself. Find your true self. Your true self is not selfish. Your true self is wise, kind and selfless and has no fear. That is your true self.

And remember, the Creator has another plan

way beyond this garbage of the universe. They will be dealt with.

That I promise you.

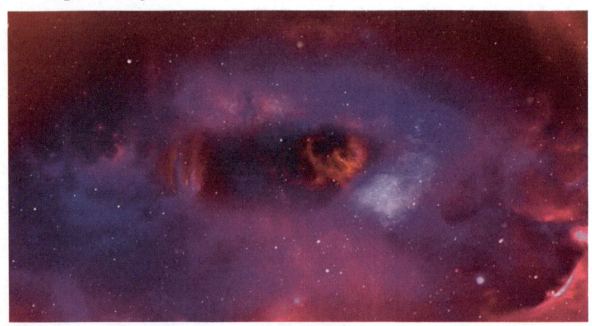

THE END

Commentary: Following April 24, 2020 Release of AI The Plan to Invade Humanity

"Within the human body of every human being is great power endowed by the Creator as we are made in the image of the Creator. Your soul, your mind, your body, your digital image, everything is interconnected to a great power that leads back to the Creator. We as a human race must upgrade our ethics and our morality and awaken through our free will alone. There is no reason for us to have fear over these garbage of the universe.

This is Cyrus A. Parsa, CEO and Founder of the AI Organization. Thank you for joining this show. I hope you liked it. It was a different perspective of the extract of the book *ARTIFICIAL INTELLIGENCE: Dangers to Humanity* and *AI, Trump, China and the Weaponization of Robotics with 5G*.

I researched and investigated over a thousand companies. So this was an extract from the of 500 Chinese companies and 600 Western, European, American companies that includes biometrics, bioengineering, cybernetics, artificial intelligence, 5G, 6G, and of course the geopolitics of our entire planet that's affecting us with this pandemic and the various other things that I called and are going to happen unless we make a huge change.

Please support me. I've done a lot of big things behind the scenes and with the help of other people as well. But on the way a lot of people, think tanks, media outlets, content creators, and people who even helped me on the way, they helped me just to get data from me so they can make content.

I really need your support. Please donate as much as you can, if you watch the movie for a price of a movie, if you enjoyed this, if it was worth something, please donate, really, really is needed. And find a link underneath or go to the website of https://TheAIOrganization.com. Subscribe and like and share everywhere.

Of course, you can take this how you like. This was fiction, or it was fact, or it was the invisible enemy. There are multiple inner meanings throughout the entire episode that I put together. All you may have at the best.
Eight months in waiting, but so many things have to be done, but the content is what's important, and the delivery of the images in the video and all the inner meanings behind them, you can use your wisdom and your knowledge to decide what's true and what's not, but what all of us need to understand

that something is very true and the Chinese Communist regime they have endangered everybody.

You're staying at home because of them. So, they must be eliminated from the entire planet and the entire universe. From the pages of time, we must expose them. That regime of China must be exposed. We can't be complicit anymore with their genocide, their persecutions, their biotech experiments, artificial intelligence, all these different things that also link back to our big tech companies who gave them these technologies.

So for our safety, for the world's safety, please help me, help us, and support The AI Organization and support me as well. Download the book *ARTIFICIAL INTELLIGENCE: Dangers to Humanity*. And that's very realistic and it takes you through different stages of present, emerging, and future threats. And roughly about 50 companies are put in that book.

The first book *AI, Trump, China and the Weaponization of Robotics with 5G* was embedded into *ARTIFICIAL INTELLIGENCE: Dangers to Humanity*. So you are welcome to just get the book *ARTIFICIAL INTELLIGENCE: Dangers to Humanity*. If you don't want to donate, just get that book from The AI Organization website or the link below.

Again, this is Cyrus A. Parsa. I hope everybody understands why I did this video and all the other videos I've done and all the articles I put together, all the books I put together and the reports I gave as well. And really, smart people you'll see the entire picture. And actually, every person and eventually we'll see the entire picture, not just what I've done, but a lot of other people have done good things as well. So, thank you. And until next time. This is Cyrus A. Parsa, The AI Organization." April 24, 2020.

CONCLUSION SECRETS EXPLAINED

The film AI The Plan to Invade Humanity you read in this storybook is in its raw original form released on April 24, 2020, including its ending narration. And I haven't changed the wordings and even the way I felt during the release of it. In fact, I stayed up 6 days straight, without sleep, to compose its images after I narrated the words for the story in one hour without stop.

The inspiration came from my 20 years of investigation and research on UFOs and classified images that I was shown of gray aliens that our military had come in contact with many years ago. Another inspirational element stemmed from the human beings replaced by Aliens disclosure with Master Li Hongzhi's 1999 Time Interview. That interview and Master Li's words was the source of the plot. And of course, the technology I developed that can scan the alien's movements played a great part in putting the plot together. I was also inspired by the notion of saving your freedoms and your lives with my exposures in preparation for the 2019 Virus outbreak and ensuing global issues. Let me explain.

I timed the movie AI: The Plan to Invade Humanity to be launched and released on April 24, 2020, via Twitter, to the President of the United States, the Pentagon, the CIA, the FBI, the NSA, Space Force, and a few special folks to create a chain reaction during lockdown. Within only 3 days of AI The Plan to Invade Humanities release, the first time in human history, the Pentagon confirmed and validated that there have been UFO landings.

Hence, the purpose of releasing this movie was multifaceted which included warning of mandated vaccines with injected nano-particles on 4-24-20 and if you paid attention, I hinted to the heart multiple times for various reasons.

Of course, the film also warned of world enslavement, lockdowns, world wars and nuclear incidents stemming from the release of the Bioweapon from the Chinese Communist Regime, and the extinction of the human race in stages, because of its corruption and complicity to the concentration camps in China. Although this movie is Sci-Fi, it is based on true events that accurately describes a horrible future unless we improve globally, become selfless and I get the support I need from a few good-hearted investors and the people to do more.

I also thought the film would bring an awakening that would reduce the conflicts during lockdown, and the potential wars, or at the very least, delay them giving everyone more chances. Basically, the first main purpose was to save lives, whether if you were liberal, conservative, rich or poor.

I Cyrus A. Parsa, the founder of The AI Organization did not have an agenda to support a side, rather to support all peoples, and save lives by bringing awareness prior to the dangerous events occurred. Of course, as you may have realized, I knew the future in detail and not just my warning of the virus in 2019, rather I was able to analyze that if I released this film during April 2020, it would lead to the beginning of declassifying our UFO files and much more.

However, there was a backstory with the reason why I released the film during that time, and the effect that it had. Because the purpose of it was to create a chain reaction from the previous disclosures I did at the time when everyone was scared in their homes, spooking the humans in the Pentagon and intelligence agencies to declassify our UFO files.

See, the months prior, and for the past previous couple years, we were noticing, especially myself, quite a bit of UFO and aliens off-world technologies landing here and entering not just the military restricted areas, but all around throughout our planet. So, my purpose initially was to create a chain reaction because many people in the Pentagon, high level generals, admirals and so on, viewed this movie, including the President of the United States, and people in Hollywood.

The script I wrote introduced a few theories never talked about before. If you consider what I did during the pandemic and the chaos of the lockdown, it was meant not just to start a chain reaction of disclosing that we've had off-world technologies land here and UFOs, and the purpose of their landings, which could be, in a sense, not positive for humanity. It was also to smash against the Alien influence and allow everyone to realize how a different time space affects us.

Since my synopsis and theory stated that the aliens were attempting to create a long-term secret invasion that takes 2 days for them, but 100 years for us, because they're in a different time space and they use quantum technology, it put the alien plot in plain view and solved a hidden mystery.

The purpose also was directed at the people who push buttons, nuclear button, as through my analysis before the pandemic happened and outbreak that I warned about I analyzed that we may have civil wars, famines, unrests, and particularly world wars having something to do with these landings and the infiltration and manipulation that we get from Aliens and Alien technology. And the stress that we may have during the pandemic.

So, I released it, so the film can penetrate the consciousness of our presidents, world leaders, and the Pentagon and so on, so they can realize and not be trigger-happy causing global wars. And not just that, because the government of China viewed this, the Russians viewed this, many agencies around the entire world viewed this movie. It did have big effects to prevent, lesson or delay great disasters that could have occurred between 2020-2022 and thereafter. Do you get it?

And if you look at the latter parts of 2020, on December 8th 2020, I did this tweet, which was a request to the President of the United States to declassify all information that we have with relation to UFOs.

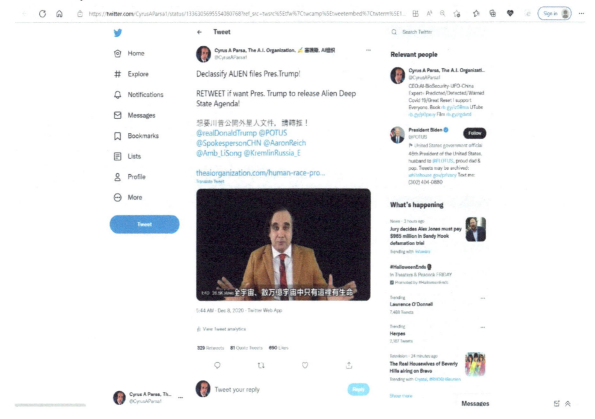

Within a few weeks, the Pentagon stated to congress that they have 6 months to declassify everything or at least start UFO disclosures at some level with the order of POTUS 45 via the December 2020 Covid Bill.

You may hate or love this picture of POTUS 45, regardless, it is history, and one is best served not being moved by emotion, rather looking at the bigger picture. UFO files began to be declassified stemming from my work here.

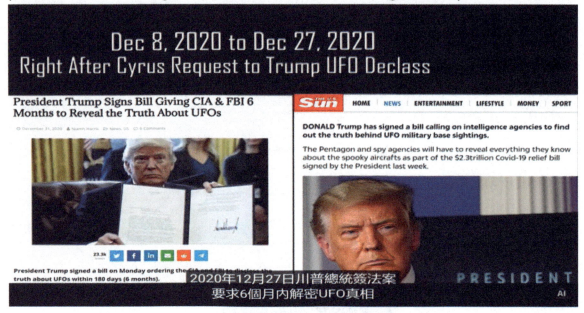

So, we're almost at that juncture. We all know how this movie affected everything. What's the possibility of the second request to President of the United States? And then a few days later, an order is put through and you have 6 months to declassify and change the history of humanity forever.

I hope everyone understands and feels why I did this movie. It was also to bring everyone together. I support particularly the positives of conservatives and liberals, really the same. Because we're all a part of the human race, we're all special. And if we're special, and we are made in an image of a higher power. And let's say these grey aliens and other aliens, they don't have our best intentions, then maybe we should consider other alternative possibilities, and be more cautious, more importantly, treat each other better. So, although this is a sci-fi movie, it is based on facts, and it was narrated in an altruistic way to build a better world.

This is Cyrus A. Parsa, The AI Organization. And I hope you not only enjoyed this film, but got some good things out of it to better not just yourself, and humanity at large. It is enough of all these fights, all these conflicts, and negativity that we've had for thousands of years. If there are trillions and trillions of planets and universes, then maybe we should consider being kinder to each other, and not being selfish but more selfless and working things out.

Although there were many brave podcasters, twitter accounts and people from the public promoting my content and warnings, there was sabotage by many others.

I want to let you the reader know, the most coordinated effort in human history by a few hundred conservative and liberal podcasters, people in Hollywood, media, social media influencers, radio talk hosts, TV hosts, reporters and their CEOs was made to censor my story, delay my disclosures, then steal its content after realizing I was right and fool the masses by either using religion on the conservative side or a platform on the liberal side while I was attempting save your freedoms and lives. Their efforts were sabotage in nature in order for them to gain a so-called perceived fame and power.

I turned down 100s of millions to the detriment of my own finances in order not to budge and make the disclosures prior to the events to reduce the damage and hurt to you, in order to save lives. If I had not done what I did, in fact it would have been 100 times worse for you. Not just with this movie, but with my federal documents on Feb 24, 2020, December 16, 2019 that reached roughly 200 nations, books on Oct 20, 2019, August 24, 2019, and Reports to Trumps Circle in summer of 2019, Reports to Fmr. CIA Covert Ops director, the Secret Service and other intelligence agencies. The efforts were not just in support of these agencies, rather you and your families.

The thing is, if your loved ones suffered from getting hit by Covid, had emotional stress from the pandemic lockdown, or lost a job or suffered from Mandated Vaccines, these people who hid my story, or plagiarized off its content hurt you and themselves, more than they hurt me because they delayed my intel, misappropriated it and went against truth, the universe. And they have created a great deal of Karma, Sin, corruption, and something that is invisible that is frightening for them and the world unless a 180 is made ASAP. Of course, those of lower capacities do not realize everything they do, think and say is watched and tallied against them.

Let me ask you. If a biological weapon was to be released on a city you lived in, and the man who worked hard to predict, detect, warn and provide solutions to save your city and your families was censored and the data stolen by your city leaders and other citizens to make money, and then your city was hit with the weapon because Cyrus was not heard, his skills not used and these guys and other citizens tried to steal the thunder and Cyrus's solutions leadings to trillions in damages, lives lost, forced mandates, famines and wars, what should be done to those guys and should Cyrus's story be made global? And why are they still making money and being followed by the masses of people? Think about it and what it means for the future.

By hiding my story, skills, and contribution and taking away support prior to the events, and to later plagiarize and attempt to take the leadership mantle, they are risking the lives of billons, you, not just themselves.

You may realize and think that it is just Pride, greed, anger, deception, Jealousy, selfishness that guides them to hurt the human race. But I will tell you, deep down it is fear, and they are controlled by an evil force to remain silent about my story and not support it in time, so it leads to deaths by

Covid, Mandated Vaccines, loss of jobs, freedoms lost, rapes, famines, murders, and world wars. Basically, for you and your loved ones to suffer and get hurt badly.

I hope you will spread this book and film far and wide by purchasing it to fund and support me and my teams in making AI The Plan to Invade Humanity into a live movie with a cast and crew for the betterment of the world. Yes, I am making it into a movie with actual people and it will be outstanding and reduce the hurt that is to come, and I need your help. Investors and public backing. Cyrus Parsa, The AI Organization

MOVIE CREATION

AI The Plan to Invade Humanity and it's one of a kind synopsis is being made into a movie by us. The script was prepared over 2 decades ago by me and formatted starting 2020 into a shooting script with the technology I created. The shooting script is a masterpiece 20 years in the making.

Support the movie creation, production, distribution, and check for updates, visit and donate to The AI Organization and God Studios, who will be one of the production companies involved along with others. Visit Theaiorganization.com and Godstudios.com and support us to make the movie happen.

GODSTUDIOS.COM

Credits

Creator of AI The Plan to Invade Humanity Film, Plot and Synopsis involving a long-term secret invasion plot by Aliens to replace, kill and extinct the human race, Powered by AI. Cyrus Parsa, The AI Organization

Images
Dreamstime.com
Motion Array

Contact.

Twitter, Instagram, Telegram, @CyrusAParsa1
Theaiorganization.com

Email Us.
Consult@theaiorganization.com

Movie
Godstudios.com

Made in the USA
Las Vegas, NV
24 November 2022